Sidekicks

D0167940

Sidekicks
ATTACK OF THE
MOLE MASTER

by Dan Danko and Tom Mason

Illustrated by Barry Gott

LITTLE, BROWN AND COMPANY

New York ⚬⚬ Boston

Little, Brown and Company

Time Warner Book Group
1271 Avenue of the Americas, New York, NY 10020
Visit our Web site at www.lb-kids.com

First Edition

ISBN 0-316-73424-1
10 9 8 7 6 5 4 3 2 1
LAKE

Printed in the United States of America

The text for this book was set in Bookman Old Style,
and the display type is Bernhard Gothic.
Book design by Billy Kelly

To Fred (every one of you)

Chapter One
The First Chapter!

"Outta the way! Outta the way!" Pumpkin Pete pounded his viney hand against the Pumpkinmobile's horn. The light turned red and Pete slammed his green, mossy foot against the gas pedal. Cars screeched to a halt as we zoomed through the intersection. A man crossing the street dove to safety as we sped by.

"Outta the way!" Pete shouted out the window. "Superhero coming through!"

I looked into the side mirror and saw the man rise to his knees and shake an angry fist.

"I don't think he's hurt," I told Pete.

"Of course he's not hurt! I'm a superhero.

And superheroes don't hurt people!" The Pumpkinmobile skidded around a corner and ran over a mailbox. Letters exploded into the air. "We *help* people." Pete slammed his fist against the horn again. "Stupid old lady! Next time I won't swerve!" he shouted at a slow-moving woman who shuffled across the street.

Twenty minutes ago, I had been polishing the chrome on the Pumpkinmobile. "Remember, wax on, wax off," Pete chuckled, and wandered into the League of Big Justice Headquarters of Big Justice. Just as I was "waxing off" the final coat, Pete raced back out into the League of Big Justice Parking Lot of Big Parking.

"Time's running out! We gotta go! No time to explain!" he called out urgently.

And now, here we were, racing off into some unknown danger against some unknown evil with the very fate of something unknown possibly hanging in some unknown balance.

That's why I love being a hero . . . or at least a superhero sidekick. I mean, come on, we punch evil in the face and stuff. Before I became a sidekick, my biggest thrill in life was sneaking into an R-rated movie. But then one day I woke up and *whammo!* I had these tiny black hairs growing in my armpits. Oh, and I could also run almost 100 miles per hour. That was three whole months ago, and now those armpit hairs are like some crazy jungle and I can run more than 110 miles per hour!

Which was about how fast my superhero sponsor, Pumpkin Pete, was driving.

"Uh . . . Pete? Maybe we should slow down?" Office buildings whizzed by in a blur.

"Oh! You'd like that, wouldn't you?"

"Yes."

"Well, we don't always get what we want! Do you think I want a big, fat, orange pumpkin for a head? Do you?!?" Pete yelled as he screeched the Pumpkinmobile around a corner.

"Actually . . . yeah, I do."

"You're darn right, I do! Because inside this big, fat, orange pumpkin head lie all the secrets of the mysterious Ways of the Pumpkin!" Pete tapped a long viney finger against his hollow gourd-head and ran another red light. "Super-hero coming through!" he shouted to the numerous skidding cars that we nearly smashed into.

"Mysterious 'Ways of the Pumpkin'?" I had never heard Pete mention them before. "What're those?"

"If I told you, there wouldn't be much mystery left, would there?"

"Maybe I should know. I *am* your sidekick. You're supposed to be training me and stuff."

"If a bomb's about to explode, whaddaya do?" Pete asked.

"Sacrifice myself for the greater good of pumpkindom," I sighed.

"That's all the training you need, Spotty."

"Speedy."

"Whatever."

I don't know how Pumpkin Pete got his pumpkin powers. For that matter, I don't even know what pumpkin powers are. "But when I decide to unleash them, all I gotta say is, stand back!" Pete always warned me. He has a large orange pumpkin for a head, so Halloween is a very traumatic time of the year for him.

That and Easter.

"The bunnies are coming! One day, you'll see!" Pete had ranted one day. "And when they come for you with those cute pink noses and fuzzy bunny paws, we'll see who's laughing then." He stared at me for a few seconds, then added, "It's me who'll be laughing. That's who. Just in case you couldn't figure that one out."

But Pete had no time for bunnies today. He looked at the Pumpkin Super Clock in the Pumpkin Super Dashboard. It was almost six o'clock.

Pete floored the Pumpkinmobile and zoomed down the road. "Come on . . . come on . . . almost there . . ."

"Where are we going, Pete? Is the League of Big Justice in trouble? Is the city threatened? Or the world? Is it the world?!? It's an invasion, isn't it? An invasion of really big nasty green bug things with big bug fangs and drool and stuff!"

"No time to talk. Must drive ridiculously fast."

We zipped around a final corner and screeched to a halt in a parking lot. I looked for the alien invasion armada, or at least some alien drool.

"Yes!" Pete rejoiced. "Two minutes to spare!" He pulled a piece of paper down from the Pumpkinmobile's sun visor and slapped it into my hand.

It was a receipt.

"Well?" Pete huffed. "You always brag about how fast you can run, but I don't see you moving so quick now!" He shooed me along with his long viney fingers. "They close at six!"

I climbed out of the Pumpkinmobile.

"And make sure they didn't shaft me on the starch," Pete yelled out the window of the Pumpkinmobile as I opened the door to the dry cleaners.

Most people think being a superhero would be cool. It probably is. I don't know. I'm just a sidekick.

Most people would think being a sidekick is cool, too. It's not. I know I thought it would be. That was before I got stuck with Pumpkin Pete.

When I first became his sidekick, he always said to me, "Remember, I'll be standing right behind you, kid." I used to think he told me that so I'd be confident in a fight against the minions of evil, knowing that my superhero sponsor was right behind me, supporting me. Truth was, Pete stood behind me so he could push me into any death trap that awaited us and run in the opposite direction.

But I guess that's just what happens when you hang out with a guy who has a big, fat, orange pumpkin for a head.

King Justice is the leader of the League of Big Justice and the total opposite of Pumpkin Pete, and by that I mean he's courageous and noble. And he doesn't have a big, fat, orange pumpkin for a head.

I've come to realize that being a sidekick is about paying your dues. And doing laundry. And washing the dishes. And waxing the Pumpkinmobile. And picking up dry cleaning.

And the Spandex? Don't even get me started on that. If you ask me, the greatest evil mastermind the world has ever known is the guy who convinced people with super powers that they had to wear brightly colored Spandex costumes and run around looking like rejects from a clown asylum.

Yeah. I wear Spandex, too. Consider it superhero peer pressure.

"We must all wear Spandex!" King Justice had informed me. "It may be butt-creeping, but it's the butt-creeping diaper of justice!"

"But evil doesn't wear Spandex."

"And that is what makes them evil!" King Justice thundered. "That and their desire to rule the world and make us all slaves."

I always wonder why evil doesn't wear Spandex. I mean, sure, you get a Spandexed villain now and then, but they're usually guys like El Poppo the Expanding Man, who had the power to expand until he popped. He didn't have much choice in clothing, unless he wanted to change his name to El Poppo the Naked Expanding Man Because All My Clothes Ripped Off.

The only other villain I know of who wore Spandex was King Nougat. He wore a peanut-colored Spandex outfit and always shouted: "Full o' chewy goodness!" which was a strange thing to yell because, technically, he was full of chewy badness.

I once asked a captured villain why so few of them wore Spandex.

"What're you, nuts?" the words exploded from his mouth. "You think we wanna run around looking like rejects from a clown asylum? I mean, have you ever taken a good look at yourself in that outfit?" He shook his head, shocked I would ask such a stupid question. "At least El Poppo the Expanding Man's got an excuse. But that goofball, Lieutenant Chew . . ."

"You mean King Nougat?" I corrected.

"Yeah! *That* guy. I don't know what the heck *he's* thinking. And technically, isn't he full of chewy *badness*?"

There was a pause. I could tell the villain was contemplating something — maybe an escape plan, perhaps his next evil idea for world domination.

"Let me ask you something," he finally said.

"Yeah?"

"What's a nougat?"

Chapter Three
I Am El Poppo!

By the way, El Poppo the Expanding Man once had a plan to hold the city for ransom. He threatened to expand until he destroyed downtown unless he was given ten million dollars.

Unfortunately for him, there are a lot of sharp corners downtown and . . . well . . .

"I'll be back! And more poppable than ever! Bwahahahaha!" he shouted as the upper half of his torso shot into the sky like a catapulted grapefruit.

I don't know what happened to King Nougat.

Chapter Four
The Chapter Before Chapter Five!

Boom Boy. Exact Change Kid. Spice Girl. Spelling Beatrice. Boy-in-the-Plastic-Bubble Boy. Charisma Kid. Earlobe Lad. And me, Speedy. We all sat in the Sidekick Super Clubhouse Room of Meetingness.

It was Saturday morning, and Exact Change Kid liked to start every sidekick meeting with roll call.

"I hereby call this official meeting of sidekicks to order!" Exact Change Kid pounded a small gavel on the table.

"Aaaaah!" Earlobe Lad screamed, and crumpled to the floor. He grabbed his large ears and balled himself up into the fetal position. "Why does everybody hate me?" he moaned.

That's something no one ever thinks about. What happens if you have a power that you can't control? I'll tell you what happens: You flop around under a table like a quivering jellyfish every time someone bangs a gavel. That was Earlobe Lad's curse: the curse of giant ears. But such is the burden of having super powers. No, not having giant ears, I mean the curse is the burden. Or maybe the burden is the curse. Oh, I don't know. It made sense when King Justice first explained it to me.

"Whose heartbeat is that? Huh? Whose is it?!?" Earlobe Lad wailed from under the table. "The pounding! The pounding! Why do you always do this to me?"

"I think he's talking about you," Spice Girl whispered to me.

"Me?" I was surprised. Or maybe I wasn't. After three months as a sidekick, the numbness was really setting in. "How do you know it's not *your* heart he's complaining about?"

"Because I do yogurt training to make my heart small," Spice Girl proudly announced.

"There are so many things wrong with that

sentence, I don't even know where to begin." I shook my head. "First of all, it's yo*ga* . . ."

"Silly! Yoga is the little green man in *E.T.*!" Spice Girl laughed.

"No, no!" Boom Boy chimed in. "Elliot was the little green man in *E.T.* Yoga was the bear."

"Mam pam pam pam mam maaaamp!" Boy-in-the-Plastic-Bubble Boy replied.

"The Ewoks?!" Exact Change Kid was shocked at Boy-in-the-Plastic-Bubble Boy's reply. "I don't think there was an Ewok named Yada."

"Wasn't Yada the alien that captured Han Solo?" Spelling Beatrice asked.

"No!" Spice Girl answered. "That was Jelly Bean."

"The pounding! The pounding!" Earlobe Lad cried out from under the table. "You're doing this just to spite me!"

Suddenly the gavel slammed against the table.

"Aaaaaaah!" Earlobe Lad screamed, and ran into the cape closet.

Charisma Kid stood at the far end of the table, gavel clenched in his hand. "I'd rather watch paint dry than spend my time with you freaks, so let's get this roll call done so I can get out of here."

Charisma Kid has great hair. He has an even greater smile. He's the sidekick to King Justice, leader of the League of Big Justice. He has all the power and confidence of a really great smile. He's the quarterback of his school football team. He was named Most Likely to Be Fallen in Love with by Every Girl in School. He is tall. He is handsome. He is athletic.

He is a jerk.

"Now that Loser Lad's gone —" Charisma Kid began.

"I heard that!" Earlobe Lad shouted from the closet.

"Let's get this over with," Charisma Kid concluded. "I have a date with myself and I hate being late."

"When I finally do blow up," Boom Boy whispered to me, "I hope I take a few of that guy's teeth with me."

"I heard that, too!" Earlobe Lad shouted.

Charisma Kid sat down like a jerk who was so satisfied that he was a jerk, he had a jerky smile that only a jerk who was so satisfied that he was a jerk would have.

Trust me, it'd make perfect sense if you saw him.

Before Charisma Kid could say another word

his perfect nose wrinkled like a cute little bunny rabbit. A cute little bunny rabbit who was a jerk, that is.

"Ugh! What's that stink? Curry and garlic?" Charisma Kid sniffed at the air.

Spice Girl looked at the ceiling and whistled.

That reminded me of this sidekick who tried to join a few weeks ago. He called himself Commander Farto: The Human Stink Bomb. He told everyone he had the power to crush evil with his overwhelming Stench of Good. We almost accepted his application, but in the end, we found out he didn't have a super power at all. He just had really, really bad gas.

"Boom Boy?" Exact Change Kid called out, continuing with roll call.

"Here!" Boom Boy replied, and raised his hand. Boom Boy has the power to blow himself up, or at least he claims to have that power. No one knows for sure if he really could. I mean, I know if that was my power, I wouldn't be too eager to blow myself up, either. So, maybe it's better to say he has the power to *threaten* to blow himself up, which really turned the tide of the battle that the Sidekicks fought against Dr. Brittle and his Delicate Army of Dainty Stained-Glass Soldiers.

"Spice Girl?"

"Here." She raised her hand as well. Spice Girl is a human spice rack. She can create any smell, or mixture of smells, with a mere thought. She isn't much good in a fight, but there's no better ally to have after Boom Boy uses the Sidekick Super Toilet of Pottiness.

"Spelling Beatrice?"

"Here." Spelling Beatrice is the oldest of the Sidekicks. Even though she's only a sidekick, she already has an archenemy: the *New York Times* crossword puzzle.

"Charisma Kid?"

"Here."

"Boy-in-the-Plastic-Bubble Boy?"

"Mpah!" I never understand a word Boy-in-the-Plastic-Bubble Boy ever says, although I have a sneaking suspicion it's probably something like, "Get me out of this big plastic hamster ball!" I have no idea how he got into his Giant Hamster Ball of Justice. I have no idea if he'll ever get out. But most important, I have no idea how he goes to the bathroom.

"Speedy?"

"Yeah," I answered. As the name suggests, I'm fast. Real fast. When I first joined the Sidekicks, there was this huge controversy over my name.

"You mean 'Speedy Kid,' right?" Exact Change Kid had asked when I first told him my sidekick name.

"No. Just Speedy," I had replied.

"That's stupid!" Boom Boy interjected. "I don't call myself 'Boom.' And hey, hey, there's 'Exact Change' and 'Earlobe.'"

"But Speedy Kid sounds lame," I defended.

"What about Speedy Boy? Or Speedy Lad? Come on! Everybody would love to be named Speedy Lad!"

"I wouldn't," I informed him.

Boom Boy stared at me. "Don't make me blow up," he threatened.

"Whoa! Whoa!" Exact Change Kid stepped between us. "There's no reason for this to get ugly. Speedy Lad obviously just doesn't understand that if you're a sidekick, you have to be a 'lad' or 'boy' or 'kid' or 'gal' or . . . or . . ."

"'Lass,'" Earlobe Lad mumbled from the other room.

"Or Lass!" Exact Change Kid agreed.

"Mmma pam pammm mam!" Boy-in-the-Plastic-Bubble Boy added.

"Exactly!" Exact Change Kid agreed. "It's just part of being a sidekick!"

"But Spelling Beatrice is just plain Spelling Beatrice!" I reminded them.

There was a pause. Boom Boy, Boy-in-the-Plastic-Bubble Boy, and Exact Change Kid exchanged uneasy looks. The closet door creaked open, and even Earlobe Lad poked his head out.

"Let's get her!" Boom Boy shouted, and everyone ran out of the room.

That was almost three months ago, and now, Exact Change Kid stopped roll call and stared across the Sidekick Super Table of Meetingness. The table is about ten feet long and oval-shaped. Each place has a small placard with a sidekick's name written on front.

"Speedy?" Exact Change Kid repeated.

"Yeah?" I repeated.

"Speedy!" Exact Change Kid said in a slightly raised voice.

"Yeah!" I yelled back even louder.

"Would somebody please shut him up?!?" Earlobe Lad cried out from the closet.

Exact Change Kid let out a sharp sigh and rolled his eyes.

"Dude. Dude," Boom Boy began, "you're supposed to say 'here.'"

"What do you mean I'm supposed to say 'here'?" I pointed at Exact Change Kid. "He knows I'm here! He's looking right at me! He's ten feet away! Who cares if I say 'here,' or 'yep,' or 'Hi-dee-yo-ho-ho'?! And why do we even take roll? There's only eight of us! But we take roll call every morning we meet. Then again after lunch. Then roll call before we go home. If we're not taking roll, then we all just sit around this table and stare at each other! We don't ever do *anything* unless the League of Big Justice calls for us. We just sit here and talk about movies we saw or some stupid TV show! What's the point? We should be training! We should be honing our battle skills! Who cares about roll call? Who cares about any of this?!?"

"Hey, hey!" Boom Boy began. "Just because you aren't going to win the Perfect Attendance Award, don't ruin it for the rest of us!"

"What Perfect Attendance Award?" I asked, afraid of the answer.

"The Perfect Attendance Award is the award you get for perfect attendance," Spice Girl informed me. "Duh."

"What does perfect attendance have to do with fighting crime?" The words burst from my mouth.

"Mamm pam pam mam maa pa! Ma maam? Pa maam? Maam mam pam ma maaam mapp paam mam ma pam," Boy-in-the-Plastic-Bubble Boy said, rolling back and forth in front of me. "Mmmm maa, pah maph paa ma. Mmaah pa phaa pam pa mmmap. Mmma pahh mm maaa pahp maaph. Maa mampm ma mmpa pamhm mahm mam pam! Maaa maaa pammm? Maa maa? Mapp pam! Ma mmmm! Mmm mamm paa! 'Pammmah pham mammph' ma ma ma pa!"

"I heard that!" Earlobe Lad shouted from the closet.

"I couldn't have said it better myself, BITPBB." Exact Change Kid patted Boy-in-the-Plastic-Bubble Boy's Giant Hamster Ball of Justice like a proud parent.

"Couldn't have said *what* better yourself?" I asked in a loud voice. "Mam pam mam pam mam mam mam?!"

"I think he said 'Mam pam mam pam mam *maa*,'" Boom Boy corrected, covering his mouth with his hand to mimic Boy-in-the-Plastic-Bubble Boy.

"Speedy, I understand you're very eager to go . . . 'fight crime' and all that," Exact Change Kid began his lecture in a slow voice. "Everybody knows how excited you are to . . . 'triumph over evil' and . . . 'save the world.' Sure, it would be great if we could spend the whole day . . . 'making the world safe' and . . . 'making the world a better place,' a world where . . . 'children could play without fear,' and we had . . . 'peace' and . . . 'understanding.' Sure that would just be swell, but while you're out gallivanting around and . . . 'helping people,' who do you think is going to be stuck back here doing all the dirty work? Hmmm? Some things are more important than that . . . 'peace on Earth' stuff."

"Like what?" I threw up my hands in frustration.

"Like what? Didn't you listen to a word Boy-in-the-Plastic-Bubble Boy said?"

I turned to Boom Boy. "Please. Blow up now. Please grab me in a bear hug and blow up."

"Hmmm," Boom Boy replied. "What's in it for me?"

"Oh, sure, being absent seems harmless enough. But one day you're skipping out on roll call and the next you're flying around the earth in your Satellite of Death, blasting countries left and right." Satisfied at his point, Exact Change Kid picked up the gavel and returned to the podium. "Trust me, it's a small step between 'tardy' and 'tyrant.'"

"Yeah! Only an 'ard' and an 'ant,'" Spice Girl chimed in. She paused. "What's an 'ard'?"

"Evil doesn't care about being tardy!" I said. "Evil doesn't give a hoot if we're absent! I'll tell you that! Evil doesn't care who's here and who's not here! It's *evil*! And it does evil things!"

"Like being absent," Spice Girl added.

Everyone was silent. Charisma Kid gave a small chuckle. No one said a word, and for a moment, I thought I had finally gotten through to them. Exact Change Kid finally looked up from the podium and stared at me.

"Speedy?" he started, lowering his pencil to the roll sheet.

I dropped my head onto the Sidekick Super Table of Meetingness with a loud thunk.

"Here," I mumbled.

Exact Change Kid smiled and happily checked off the empty box next to the name "Speedy Lad."

"Earlobe Lad?" he continued.

"Here," his voice called out from the cape closet.

And then we all sat there, staring at each other.

"So," Spice Girl said after an eternity of silence. "Anyone seen any good movies lately?"

Chapter Five
Chapter Five!

The clock struck 11:00.

"Anybody want some pizza?" Spelling Beatrice asked.

"Mmma pam maa!" Boy-in-the-Plastic-Bubble Boy called out.

"Yeah, I hate olives, too," Exact Change Kid agreed.

"Hey, hey! Why don't we go to Pizza World? They give a Superhero Discount," Boom Boy suggested.

"But we're only sidekicks," Spice Girl reminded him.

"No one has to tell *them* that!" Boom Boy replied.

"But before we go," Exact Change Kid began. "Let's take a quick roll call. Boy-in-the-Plastic-Bubble Boy?"

"Mamp!"

I dropped my head on the table with a loud *thunk*. Again.

"Boom Boy?"

"Here."

"Earlobe Lad?"

"Here," his voice called out from the closet.

Chapter Six
The Sixth Chapter, in Which Foreshadowing Is Used Once Again to Tease the Readers So They Shall Buy the Next Sidekicks Book

"What are they doing now?" the voice asked.

"Eating pizza," the minion replied.

"Pizza?"

"Yes. Pizza."

"I see."

There was a moment of silence while the voice considered the possibilities.

"What kind of pizza?" the voice finally asked.

"We're not sure, but there are no olives."

"I see."

Again, silence. The voice had not foreseen this eventuality. There was a reason. There must be. If only the voice could crack the enigma of this event.

"Where are they eating the pizza?" the voice finally asked.

"Pizza World, we believe."

"I see."

Possibilities, endless possibilities unfolded like an onion smashed against a wall.

"They ordered the pizza and received the 'Superheroes Discount,'" the minion revealed.

"Superheroes Discount? They're not superheroes! They're just sidekicks!"

"By our records, yes."

"What kind of sidekicks pretend they're superheroes to get a discount on their pizza?"

"Bad sidekicks, O great leader. Bad sidekicks."

"Of all the irresponsible things I've ever heard! When I rule the world, I'll have a thing or two to say to the League of Big Justice about teaching honesty, I'll tell you that much!"

"Will you tell them your ideas on honesty before or after you destroy the Sidekicks?"

The voice thought for a moment, considering the multitude of options like a master studying a chessboard.

"After. That way I can blame it on them."

"Sure, sure. All kinds of super powers."

The girls giggled.

"I can fly. And I'm super strong. And rays come out my eyes."

The girls gasped.

"Sure, sure. Rays. Right out of my eyes. Just when evil thinks it's going to win . . . *blammo!* I zap 'em with my laser eyes!"

The girls flinched. Boom Boy sat back in the Pizza World booth and gave a satisfied nod.

"Yep, yep," Boom Boy sighed. "When evil sees me coming, it's time to cry for mommy."

"Evil has a mommy?" the blond girl asked.

"Oh sure, sure," Boom Boy replied. "A very evil mommy."

The other girl turned to Exact Change Kid. "What powers do you have?"

"I . . . I . . . I . . . I . . . ," Exact Change Kid nervously stammered as he stared into her beautiful green eyes.

"He's an alien," Boom Boy jumped in. "A very stupid alien who was sent to Earth because he was so stupid. He doesn't understand English." Boom Boy turned to Exact Change Kid and said in a very loud, slow voice, "YOU WANNA EATTA MORE PIZZA? YUMMY, YUMMY?"

Exact Change Kid slumped in the booth like a deflated balloon that was sent to Earth from another planet of balloons because he was so stupid. "Yes," he mumbled. "Me eatta more."

The blond girl looked at Earlobe Lad. Beads of sweat ran down his forehead as he summoned every ounce of willpower he had to shut out the two girls' happy giggles and cheerful voices. But then, I wasn't sure if the sweat was from the severe pain that stabbed at Earlobe Lad's massively sensitive eardrums or the absolute terror he felt at talking to two cute girls.

"Why are you sweating?" the blonde girl said to Earlobe Lad.

"It's my super power," Earlobe Lad whispered. "I'm Captain . . . Sweat Man. And my super power is to sweat. A lot."

"Is that really a power?" the girl with green eyes asked.

"Sure," Earlobe Lad murmured. "I . . . sweat . . . on the forces of evil and sting them with my . . . salty goodness."

"You have big ears!" The green-eyed girl squealed with delight.

Earlobe Lad's eyes bulged from his head. His left eye twitched as if a tiny earthquake rattled through his brain. He leaned against the table and did all he could to not crumble to the floor and quiver like a mass of Jell-O.

Just like he always did when he was faced with the terrifying sounds of fun and laughter.

"The funny thing is," Boom Boy jumped in, "even though he's got giant ears, he's really hard of hearing. So speak really, really LOUD."

Earlobe Lad dug his fingers into the booth's upholstery and prepared for the tidal wave of sound that was about to smash into his huge-eared head. Boom Boy chuckled, pleased with the brilliance of his practical joke.

The blond girl took a deep breath and opened her mouth, but before a single shouted word passed her lips, Earlobe Lad slid beneath the table and rolled into a trembling ball. "Why does everyone hate me?" he whined.

With an open seat now at the table, Boy-in-the-Plastic-Bubble Boy quickly rolled over to Boom Boy and the two girls.

"Mam mam paaahm mam pa?" he said, leaning against the inside of his Giant Hamster Ball of Justice and giving a sly wink to the blond girl.

I sat in the next booth with Spice Girl and Spelling Beatrice. We watched the whole, sad drama while eating our pizza. For some reason, it reminded me of the time Pumpkin Pete tried to buy a top hat to go with his tuxedo. Sure, it was funny to watch, but in the end, you just felt a little disturbed.

Except for Charisma Kid, who had hurried off for his big date with himself, all of us had followed Boom Boy's suggestion and headed to Pizza World for lunch. And, as he said he would, Boom Boy claimed we were all superheroes, and we got a ten percent discount. The moment the two girls heard we were "superheroes," they tripped over each other to talk to Boom Boy.

Spelling Beatrice shook her head about Earlobe Lad. "That wasn't very nice of Boom Boy."

"What'd you expect? Those two are always at it," I reminded her.

"Maybe he's recharging his sweat powers," Spice Girl theorized, leaning out of our booth to see Earlobe Lad huddled beneath the next table. She gave him a happy little finger wave and then leaned back into the booth. "And all this time I thought he had giant ears."

"He does have giant ears," I reminded her.

"I know," she said, and took a bite of pizza. "And that's what makes him so sweaty."

I looked at Spelling Beatrice. She just shrugged her shoulders and took a gulp of soda.

"Why do you want to be sidekicks?" I asked them. The question had been bothering me for some time, and I knew Spelling Beatrice would be the one sidekick who could give me something that actually resembled a sane answer.

Spelling Beatrice thought for a moment. "I never told anyone this, but my real parents . . . well . . . they were killed in a freak spelling accident. And when my Grammar Powers first developed, I swore that no innocent would ever fall before the dark side of phonetics again."

Did I say *sane*?

"A . . . *spelling* accident?" I asked.

"Yes. To this day, I still can't look at umlauts without getting teary-eyed."

"Don't be sad. I don't like eggs, either." Spice Girl offered a sympathetic hand. "I thought this was Math Club. Then everybody looked funny and did funny things!"

"Wait. You mean you didn't know this was a group of superhero sidekicks when you joined?" I couldn't believe it.

"No, I didn't. But that's okay. I don't know anything about math, either."

"How about you, Speedy? Why did you want to become a sidekick?" Spelling Beatrice asked.

"I thought . . . I dunno. I thought it'd be cool. I thought maybe I could use my speed and stuff to make a difference. I mean, what else was I going to do? I always wanted to be a superhero, and then one day I woke up and could run faster than a car. That's pretty scary stuff."

"It's nice to know there's other people like you, huh?" Spelling Beatrice replied. "It's nice to know you're not alone."

I had never thought about it until that moment. Maybe that's why I put up with all the craziness and the dishwashing and dirty laundry. Sure, it was great to save the earth now and then, but it was also great to feel a *part* of something, you know? Something bigger than you. Something . . . something better than you. Something that makes you feel like you're part of a . . . a family.

A family of mutated oddities with huge ears, unbelievable grammar, exact change, and plastic bubbles, but a family nonetheless.

It made me think about my real family. They never say it, but I always feel my mom and dad are embarrassed about my super powers. My brother is "normal." As a florist, the only super power he has is the ability to make a killer centerpiece for the head table at a wedding.

My mom has a very strict rule of "no super powers in the house." And my dad? Sometimes he acts like he's working up the nerve to have "the talk" with me. You know the one I'm talking about. But instead of it being about the birds and the bees, it's gonna be about Spandex and the dangers of Kryptonite.

The thing that really started to bug me the most? At that moment, I really didn't know if it was my parents who thought I was a freak, or if it was me.

"I was thinking that maybe we sidekicks

should do a little more training? In *theory*, we're going to be members of the League of Big Justice someday."

Spelling Beatrice nodded. "What were you thinking?"

"It'd probably be helpful if we knew how to fight, don't you think? And maybe some strategy training? And maybe one of us should know how to fly the League of Big Justice Super Jet of . . . Superness or whatever they call that thing."

"Oh! Oh! I know what we can do!" Spice Girl gushed. "Let's have a family picnic!"

"That's not exactly what I had in mind."

"We can train for the three-legged race. And train for the pie-eating contest. And even train to bob for apples! That's a lot of training!" Spice Girl explained. "Or did you mean 'train,' like a choo-choo?"

"A family picnic?!" I snorted. "I'd rather be trapped in Boy-in-the-Plastic-Bubble Boy's Giant Hamster Ball of Justice with Earlobe Lad than have a family picnic!"

"I heard that!" Earlobe Lad moaned from under the table.

"All right! Which one of you jokers claimed to be a superhero to get a discount?" a Pizza World employee asked as he walked up.

Pumpkin Pete suddenly burst from the booth behind us. He held a large pizza box under his arm and bolted for the front door. "Pumpkin feets, don't fail me now!" he shouted as he raced from Pizza World.

The Pizza World employee was about sixteen years old and had an oddly large head. His black hair was riddled with dandruff, as if he had his own personal snowstorm following him around. "You can't fool me. You're not superheroes! You're just a bunch of sidekicks!"

Exact Change Kid went pale. "Now I'll never get into Harvard," he whispered.

"Stay cool. Stay cool," Boom Boy whispered back. He turned to the Pizza World employee and said in a deep, booming voice, "Beware, citizen! You know not what forces with which you toy!"

"Ooooo! What're you going to do? Threaten to blow up?" The Pizza World employee laughed.

Boom Boy was stunned. "He knows all our deadliest secrets! Who are you?"

"Maybe this will rattle the cobwebs from your memory!" the Pizza World employee warned. He bent over and balled his fists.

"It's Boom Boy's evil twin!" Spice Girl called out.

The Pizza World employee's face turned red,

and it was followed by an explosion. A small, very stinky explosion.

Earlobe Lad peered out from under the table. "Hey! I know you!" he whispered as loud as he could stand. "You're that Commandant Poop guy!"

The Pizza World employee struck a dramatic pose and puffed out his chest. "That's Commander Farto: The Human Stink Bomb! Ever since you kicked me out of the Sidekicks, I've waited for this day! And now, revenge shall be mine! You liars owe us three dollars and seventy-eight cents!"

"Run away!" Exact Change Kid yelled.

Everyone burst from the two booths and did their best impression of Pumpkin Pete.

"Laugh while you can, sidekicks! By all that's smelly, I swear as long as there is gas in my bowels, my time shall come, and you will rue the day you dared turn your back on Commander Farto: The Hu —"

"Hey! Farthead!" The manager walked up with a mop. "Someone stuffed a calzone down the toilet and flooded the bathroom."

He shoved the mop into Commander Farto's shaking hand and walked back to the cash register.

"Laugh while you can, Pizza World manager!"

Commander Farto said in a low, angry voice. "By all that's smelly, I swear as long as there is gas in my bowels, my time shall come, and you will rue the day you dared give toilet duty to Commander Farto: The Human Stink Bomb!"

Chapter Eight
Nooooooooooooooo!

"A family picnic?" Exact Change Kid clapped his hands together. "That's a terrific idea!"

Noooooooooooooo!

Chapter Nine
Noooooooooooooooo! Part II

"A family picnic?" King Justice clapped his hands together. "That's a terrific idea!"

Noooooooooooooooo!

Chapter Ten
A Glimmer of Hope!

"A family picnic?" My mom scratched her chin. "It sounds dangerous. I don't know if your father would approve . . ."

Yes!

"A family picnic?" My dad clapped his hands together. "That's a terrific idea!"

Noooooooooooooooo!

Chapter Twelve
Noooooooooooooooo! Part IV

"All those who wish to compete in the father-son three-legged race, please come to the starting line!" a voice boomed over the loudspeaker.

"I don't want to enter. We'll just lose," I complained.

"Where there is hope, where there is strength, the impossible can become! The! Ordinary!" King Justice proclaimed. "Go forth and bind your leg to yonder father with courage, young Speedy!"

"I'm up for it if you are, son," my dad stated as I walked up to him.

"I'm over here, Dad," I replied.

"Where?"

"Here."

"Say something again."

"Here."

My dad rotated left, then right, then finally turned in the right direction . . . if I had been on the other side of him.

"No, Dad. I'm over *here*."

The one good thing about being evil is that you probably don't spend very much time with your kids. I mean, you're busy building death rays and creating plots to rule the world, and that's all very time-consuming. Hardly leaves weekends to play catch and stuff.

And on days like this, I really wish my parents were evil, because if they were, then they'd be out putting the finishing touches on their Satellite of Doom instead of dragging me along to the League of Big Justice Super Family Picnic of Potluck.

Everyone was there. Unfortunately. King Justice, Mr. Ironic, Captain Haggis, The Good Egg, Depression Dave, Lady Bug, The Stain, The Librarian, and Pumpkin Pete. Only Ms. Mime was missing. Her name was "mysteriously" deleted from the League of Big Justice's Super Computer of Justice's League of Big Justice Super Family Picnic of Potluck Invitation List of Justiceness, or something.

Apparently, even the earth's mightiest heroes hate mimes.

It was supposed to be "a chance for the dull, ordinary schlubs who ride the bus to work each day in their pathetic little lives to rub elbows with greatness." At least that's how Pumpkin Pete had described it when I first told him about it.

All the Sidekicks attended, decked out in their full costumes. The problem was, since all the heroes and sidekicks had secret identities, we had to protect our families' identities. So the parents of all the Sidekicks had to conceal their identities so no one knew who they were.

"It would be just like evil to attack during the amazing enjoyability of Farmer Dupree's Family Hayride!" King Justice had said when he handed an Identity Containment Apparatus to each sidekick. "Make certain your parents wear these ICAs. The very future of their boring, uneventful, super power–less lives may! Be! At! Stake!"

"Uh . . . King Justice?" I began, taking two for my parents. "These are just brown paper bags."

"Oh, there's more to those bags than just paper and brown, my doubting little speed moppet!" King Justice replied.

"Like what?" I asked.

"Like asbestos! Such! A! Deal! At the government surplus store . . . and they're flame-retardant."

"I think they prefer to be called 'fire challenged,'" Spice Girl corrected.

So there I was in the park with my parents, both wearing paper bags over their heads like they were embarrassed to be seen with me. Well, the joke was on them because no one could've been more embarrassed than I was at that moment.

"So, when's this three-legged race start?" Pumpkin Pete asked, walking up to my dad and me.

"Right after lunch," I replied.

"I don't think we've met. I'm Pumpkin Pete. I have all the powers of a Pumpkin."

"I know, Pete," I sighed. "I'm your sidekick."

"Hey! I thought I recognized you!" Pete spouted and slapped me on the back. "So . . . so . . . good to see you're still . . ."

"Alive?" I finished.

"Yeah, yeah," Pete agreed.

There was an awkward pause. Pete looked at the ground and shuffled one foot in the grass.

"You're probably wondering how I escaped

the explosion zone of the anti-Earth dimension last month," I finally said, breaking the silence.

"Actually, I was really wondering if anyone would notice I just brought a can of Cheez Whiz for the potluck." Pete held out an old can of Cheez Whiz. Dried orange "cheese" was crusted around the spout. "But now that you mention it, I am a little curious how you survived." Pete put the Cheez Whiz tip in his mouth and began sucking cheese as he listened.

"Well, after you pushed me into the trans-dimensional vortex, I —"

"What? *Pushed* you? Did my big, fat, orange pumpkin ears hear you right? *Pushed* you?" Pete protested, bits of gooey Cheez Whiz flying from his mouth.

"After Dr. Draino opened the vortex, you pushed me in the back and ran the other way," I reminded him.

"No, no, no! That's what we superheroes call a distraction. A *super* distraction. You've got a lot to learn, kid." Pete shook his head in disgust. "*Pfft*. These sidekicks . . ."

"You yelled, 'Pumpkin feets, don't fail me now!' and ran away. How is *that* a distraction?" I challenged.

"I'm alive, aren't I?" Pete replied.

"Yes."

"And *you're* alive, aren't you?"

"Yes."

"And Dr. Draino is trapped in the anti-Earth dimension, isn't he?"

"Yes."

"Then chalk one up for the superhero with the big, fat, orange pumpkin head and zero for Captain Complain-O Jr.," Pete concluded. He jabbed the Cheez Whiz tip back in his mouth and gave a triumphant suck.

I don't know why I even bother.

"Anyway, I defeated Dr. Draino and found a way back to this dimension," I hastily said.

"Good for you, but don't think you're gonna be so lucky in the three-legged race, Complain-O Jr." Pete held up a mannequin that had one leg tied to his own. The mannequin's head was missing and an orange basketball had been shoved onto its neck. "Me and my boy here are gonna mop up the floor with you two."

"*That's* your son? It's just a mannequin with a basketball for a head," I pointed out.

Pete gasped and threw his arms up in the air. "Hey! I don't call your son a blockhead!"

"I don't have a son, Pete. I'm thirteen."

"Hey! Hey!" It was Boom Boy, guiding his father by the hand. "This is my dad. Or maybe my mom." Boom Boy peeked under the bag that covered his parent's head. "Yep. Dad."

"It's nice to meet you," Boom Boy's dad said, holding his hand out toward Pumpkin Pete's mannequin. "So, what's everyone doing?"

"We're just getting ready for the three-legged race," I said.

"Oh, I see how it is," Boom Boy's dad began. "Don't tell Boom Boy and Boom Boy's dad so they don't have a chance to win the three-legged race. So that's how it's going to be, is it?"

"But we're telling you now . . . uh . . . Boom Boy's . . . dad," I told him.

"'Cause you knew if you didn't . . . if you didn't . . . I swear, I'd blow myself up!" Boom Boy's dad shouted. He doubled over and clenched his fists.

"Go on, dad! Show 'em what happens when they mess with us!" Boom Boy cheered.

"What's going on, son?" my dad asked, hearing the grunts and groans.

"It's a long story," I sighed.

"I'll bet you five hundred bucks his head flies

the farthest," Pete said, holding out an orange bill with an image of a black train.

"That's Monopoly money," I pointed out.

"Monopoly money, or my ticket to Boardwalk?" Pete huffed.

"You can do it this time, Dad! I know you can!" Boom Boy urged him. "Blow up real good!"

In response to his son's encouragement, Boom Boy's dad grunted louder and curled into a fetal position, like a big baby with a brown bag on its head trying to blow up.

"Uh . . . Mr. Pumpkin? Since you're a superhero and all, shouldn't you be stopping this?" my dad asked.

"Hey, Brown-Bag-Head-Guy, once this other Brown-Bag-Head-Guy is gone, all I have to do is get rid of you and your blockhead son and this race is mine!" Pete informed us.

"Wait!" Boom Boy's dad said. He unballed his fists and stood up. "I get it now. I get it. You *want* me to blow up, don't you?"

"Actually, yeah," Pumpkin Pete confessed.

"I bet! 'Cause once I do, I'll be gone and then there'll be no more Boom Boy's dad to win the three-legged race with Boom Boy!"

"Look, the race won't even start for twenty

56

minutes," I reminded Boom Boy's dad. "You can still enter."

"And that's how it better stay, because if I find out it's too late . . . I swear, I swear I'll blow myself up!" Boom Boy's dad threatened.

"Yeah, yeah! Me, too!" Boom Boy joined his father. "We'll *both* blow up!"

"Well, I wish one of you would blow up so I can win this stupid race," Pumpkin Pete grumbled. "The winner gets a cheese basket. I like cheese."

Boom Boy looked at Pumpkin Pete. "Win the race? Your kid's just a mannequin with a basketball for a head."

"Hey! I don't call your son a blockhead!" Pete yelled.

"I don't have a son, Pete. I'm fourteen," Boom Boy responded.

"Dad? Can we please go?" I asked. I had been down this road before and didn't like the scenery much the first time.

"What about the race?"

"If it's like anything else the Sidekicks do, trust me when I say it'll never happen. I guarantee you, any second now, Exact Change Kid is going to show up to discuss the rules."

"Since we have a little time before the race, I'd thought we should discuss the rules." Exact Change Kid strolled up and dropped a book thicker than the phone book at his feet.

Pete pulled Exact Change Kid aside. "Does it say anything in there about kids who are physically . . . uh . . . impaired?"

"Exactly what kind of impairment?" Exact Change Kid returned a sideways glance.

"Oh . . . I don't know," Pete whispered back. "Like . . . say . . . having a basketball for a head?"

I escaped with my dad to the picnic table where my mom sat with some of the other sidekicks' parents. Maybe there were some brothers and sisters there, too. Or even a cousin. I have no idea. They all had bags over their heads.

"Hey, honey," Dad said, talking to an ice chest.

I sat next to my mom and noticed that a lady wearing a brown bag over her head was lying on the ground. Her fists were balled and she was grunting like a wrestler.

"Who's she?" I asked my mom.

"I'm really not sure," she began. "I just told her I was entering my pie in the dessert contest, and suddenly she fell on the ground and started grunting."

My dad had finished his conversation with

the ice chest and was shuffling toward my mom and me, both hands extended out like he was playing blindman's bluff.

"Careful, Dad," I warned him, pointing to the woman rolling on the ground. "You almost stepped on Boom Boy's mother."

"Mmmm! This is such an interesting dish, Captain Haggis," my mom said, doing the best she could to move the fork underneath the paper bag without poking herself in the chin. "What do you call it again? Haggis?"

"Aye!" Captain Haggis replied. "Thet's me family specialty ya got there, ma'am."

"Tell me there's no milk in it!" King Justice interrupted. "I'm lactose intolerant and it'll make me get all poopy!"

"Nigh, she ain't got none inner."

"Foul lactose demon! You'll not have me on this day!" King Justice called out, and he shoveled another large spoonful into his mouth.

"I'd love to get the recipe." My mom moved another spoonful under her bag.

"Sure 'nuff missus," Captain Haggis proudly responded, and wiped some haggis from his wild beard. He laid his bagpipes on the ground and leaned forward on the table. "Wahl, first ye get yerself a wee little lamb."

"Oh good! I just love lamb!" my mom enthused.

"Than, ya take th' little feller's heart, an' ya chop it up and stuff it inna th' feller's stomach. Than ya take the little feller's lungs, ya chop 'em up an' stuff 'em inna th' stomach, tew. Than ya take yer hand an' ya dig 'round real deep insigh' th' little feller an' get yerself a good fistful a' fat. Ya take tha' fat an' ya chop it up an' stuff it inna th' stomach, tew. An' while yer at it, ya might as well chop up th' intestine, kidney an' liver, an' stuff 'em inna th' stomach, tew."

A choking noise came from under my mom's paper bag. Everybody at the picnic table slowly lowered their forks and spoons.

"You gonna finish that?" Pumpkin Pete asked, wrapping a long viney finger around my mom's bowl of haggis.

"No . . . no," she slowly answered. "It's all yours."

"More for me!" Pete shoved another huge spoonful of haggis into his mouth.

Mr. Ironic looked down on his half-eaten bowl of haggis. "We ate it with the expectation of a potluck treat, and yet, here we are, having learned the terrible truth. Now, nothing is left in our mouths but the bitter taste of . . . irony."

"I feel all poopy," King Justice grumbled. He rubbed his tummy and pushed away his bowl of haggis.

"Anyway, once ya get all thet inna th' wee stomach," Captain Haggis continued, "ya take a big bag o' oatmeal an —"

"OATMEAL!?" Pete shouted, and spat out a mouthful of haggis. "I *hate* oatmeal!"

"Sorry we're late!" Spice Girl called out as she came up to the picnic table with her parents.

Spice Girl had a brown paper bag on her head.

"Why are you wearing an Identity Containment Apparatus?" I asked.

"Wearing what?" she responded.

"An Identity Containment Apparatus?" I restated.

"Oh, that!" Spice Girl laughed. "You want to know why I'm wearing the Identity Containment Apparatus?"

"Yes!"

"Well . . . it's because I . . ." She paused. "What's an Identity Containment Apparatus?"

I let out a long sigh. "Why are you wearing the paper bag on your head?"

"Oh *that* Identity Containment Apparatus! It's to protect my identity, silly!"

"It's supposed to protect your *parents'* identities! We all know you're Spice Girl," I explained.

"Who told you?" she gasped.

"For one, you're wearing your pink sidekick outfit that says 'Girl Power,'" I informed her. "And for two, you smell like coriander."

"Oh! Like this . . . this Spice Girl person you keep talking about is the *only* one who smells like coriander?"

"Uh . . . yes, she is."

"Well, if I see this 'Spice Girl,'" she raised both her hands and made air quotes with her fingers, "I'll tell her you said 'Hi.'"

"Hi, Spice Girl!" Boom Boy strolled up. "What's with the bag?"

Spice Girl slumped. A sniffle came from under her Identity Containment Apparatus.

"Don't worry, sweetheart. I'll take care of this," Spice Girl's mother whispered to her and turned to face me.

"Hello. I'm not Spice Girl's mother. It's a pleasure to meet you." Spice Girl's mother motioned to her husband. "And this isn't Spice Girl's father . . ."

"Hi. Hi," Spice Girl's father said, shaking my hand. "My name's Stev —"

Spice Girl's mother gave him a sharp elbow.

"I mean . . . my name's . . . Joey. Joey Joe Joe Junior . . . Shabadoo."

"My real last name's *Shabadoo*?" Spice Girl was dazed. "I'm sad now."

"If that was my last name, I'd blow up for sure," Boom Boy whispered.

"I know this is a family picnic and all, but maybe now is a good time to take roll call," Exact Change Kid strolled up and suggested.

"Don't you have any pennies to sort?" I huffed.

"Nope. I'm all done." To prove his accomplishment, Exact Change Kid produced five stacks of pennies. "Sorted by date and U.S. mint," he boasted.

Exact Change Kid pushed his glasses up his nose and smiled. "Abe and I have been through a lot of battles," he added, sliding the coins into the change dispenser on his waist. Exact Change Kid stepped onto a nearby rock and struck a heroic pose, standing tall in the face of adversity. "I'll tell you, Speedy Lad, some may fight crime with super strength . . . with super speed . . . with so-called super *powers*, but there is nothing more powerful than the tiny little heads stamped on these coins. Lincoln, Roosevelt, Washington, Jefferson, Kennedy, Susan B. Anthony — these are my agents of justice, my Powers of Legal U.S. Tender. Wherever an innocent needs exact change to ride a bus, when the helpless cry out at a parking meter, when good stands alone at a pay phone, that's where you'll find me, Speedy. That's where you'll find *me*."

"What a hero. . . ." My mom's admiration was matched only by my disdain.

"Mom! He throws pennies!"

"Yes, son, but he throws them at evil."

"Mamm pamm pamam maa maa!" Boy-in-the-Plastic-Bubble Boy called out as he rolled up with his parents. His Giant Hamster Ball of Justice banged repeatedly against the picnic table, and he continued with "Paaam maam ma pa paaam mammmm!"

Boy-in-the-Plastic-Bubble Boy's dad grabbed me by the wrist. He pulled me to his side; his grip was tight, and I could see a slight tremble in his arm.

"Please . . . help us . . . ," he whispered in a

tired and fearful voice, his breath heavy against the inside of the paper bag that covered his head. "We can't understand anything he says! He just runs around the house in that . . . in that bowling ball saying 'mamm pamm pa ma maamm'! What's a 'mamm pamm'? For the love of my sanity, tell me what a mamm pamm is!"

Boy-in-the-Plastic-Bubble Boy rolled up to his dad. "Maamm paam?" he asked.

"Yes son. Maamm . . . paam . . . ," Boy-in-the-Plastic-Bubble Boy's dad replied in a slow, cracking voice. "Maamm . . . paam . . ."

"Who wants dessert?" My mom pulled out two large Tupperware bowls. "I made a nice pumpkin pie —"

"AAAAAAAAAH!" Pumpkin Pete screamed, and grabbed his head. "You monster!"

Pete jumped up and fled the table. The mannequin tied to his leg broke in half. Pete raced away with the mannequin's upper torso dragging behind him. "Run! Run! She'll cook us all!" Pete shouted in blind panic and dove behind a large lilac bush.

King Justice leaned across the table and whispered, "There's not a chance that other container has egg salad, is there?"

A single tear ran down The Good Egg's cheek as he waited, filled with dread, at my mom's fateful answer.

"I'll just go put these in the car," my mom said, grabbing both Tupperware bowls. She walked ten feet and directly into a tree.

I stood up from the table to help her when a man stomped over with his young son. "All right! Which one of you Halloween rejects stole my kid's ball?" the angry man yelled. "Come on, who stole my son's basketball?"

There was a long silence. All the members of the League of Big Justice and the Sidekicks averted their eyes.

Suddenly, from behind the lilac bush, a voice shouted, "Your son's a blockhead!"

Chapter Fourteen
I Am the Egg Man

"And then what happened?" Miles asked.

"King Justice made Pete give the kid back his basketball, but it had a big hole in it from the mannequin's neck, so the kid cried," I replied. "Then the attack happened."

"Attack? You guys were attacked?"

"Yeah. Ants. Millions of 'em. King Justice called a retreat and everyone ran back to their cars."

"Were they giant mutant monster ants?"

"No. Tiny black ones in the park."

"Wow," Miles was amazed. "Earth's greatest heroes defeated by ants."

"These weren't ordinary ants!" I defended.

"They were all attitude, and man, could they bite!"

We sat on the bleachers and watched football tryouts. Miles wanted to sign up for the team. He was a little chubby and could barely manage to chew gum and walk at the same time. He was a shoe-in for team statistician.

"I'll score touchdowns with a pencil!" Miles boasted.

I went with him because he was my best friend and we always hung out together when I wasn't sidekicking. The fact that Prudence Cane was a cheerleader and would be at the tryouts as well was sheer coincidence.

Yeah. Right.

Prudence is so beautiful, she would even look good in Spandex, unless it was pulled over her head. Then she would just look stupid. If Prudence were a banana split, she'd be four blond scoops of vanilla with a bucket of hot fudge and a mountain of nuts. But she wouldn't be sticky. And she would never, ever melt.

Prudence and I play this funny game we made up. I pretend that I'm madly in love with her, and she pretends to not know that I even exist. Unfortunately, she's very, very good at it.

"Hey, Prudence," I said as Miles and I walked down the sidelines.

"Hey . . ."

"Guy."

"Yeah. Guy." Prudence sized me up. "Do I know you?"

"I sit next to you in Algebra!"

"Ethel Murdock sits next to me."

"I'm on the other side."

"Oh. I never look that way," Prudence informed me. "That's the boring side of the room."

Silence. My heart pounded so loud, Earlobe Lad's head would have exploded if he were there.

"So . . . ," I began, fighting the awkwardness. "Nice pom-poms."

The moment the words left my mouth, I wished silently for a massive alien invasion to end my suffering. A giant laser blast, or maybe a disintegration ray. Anything. Anything to alter the current reality in which I was a complete idiot. The other cheerleaders snorted and held back laughter. Prudence gave them an uncomfortable look — a "get me outta here" look.

"Uh . . . thanks," she said against the backdrop of giggling cheerleaders, and gently shook a blue pom-pom. She was the captain and was the only one with blue pom-poms. The other girls had red, but who cares about them?

See, the thing is, if that alien ship came and started blasting the football field, I'd have a reason to use my powers. I'd save Prudence. I'd defeat the aliens. I'd save the school.

Well, maybe two out of three.

And then, as the alien mothership turned tail and ran away into hyperspace, Prudence would look at me and say, "You are the bravest, most handsome and wonderful sidekick in the world!"

But there are two problems with that little scenario.

Problem #1: No matter how hard I looked at the cloudy sky, no alien invasion came.

Problem #2: When I became a sidekick, I promised King Justice that I would be responsible with my powers. I swore an oath to never abuse my powers for personal gain.

Stupid oaths.

"Well, well. Looks like the team's got a new waterboy," a voice behind me said. I didn't need to turn around, I could recognize the syrup that oozed from each word.

Mandrake Steel, a.k.a. Charisma Kid.

When I mentioned that Charisma Kid was

quarterback for his school football team, did I mention it was *my* school football team as well?

"Hi, Mandrake!" Prudence gushed.

"Nice pom-poms," Mandrake replied.

Prudence nearly swooned. All the cheerleaders sighed and batted their eyelashes.

"That's so sweet of you!" Prudence smiled.

Come on! Come on! There's got to be aliens up there somewhere, just waiting to zoom down and blast us!

"What're you doing here?" Mandrake asked me. "You're not trying out for the team?"

"No, *I* am!" Miles spoke up.

Mandrake gave Miles the once-over and laughed. "What position?"

"Statistician!" Miles proudly announced.

"And I suppose you're going to be chief eraserhead?" Mandrake asked me.

I didn't reply. When he was in his Charisma Kid identity, Mandrake was still a jerk, but he was a jerk on the side of good. He was smarmy. He was egotistical. But he was still a hero. He poked fun at me and the Sidekicks, but we knew, when it came to punching evil in the face, he was knuckle-to-knuckle with us.

But when he was just "normal" Mandrake . . .

it seemed he made up for all the goodness he did as Charisma Kid. Nothing made Mandrake Steel happier than making Guy Martin miserable.

Unfortunately, *I'm* Guy Martin.

"Or maybe you could be vice president in charge of tying my shoes?" he continued.

My face turned beet red and my hand balled into a fist. I wasn't afraid of Mandrake. Far from it. But I was afraid of his popularity. One wrong move against Mandrake would make me as popular as a zit on prom night.

"Don't push me," I warned.

"And what if I do?" he replied, and pushed me.

I've fought madmen and mad scientists, supervillains and super computers, giant monsters and giant robots, and never once, not once, did I feel as helpless as I did now. Mandrake was right. What could I do? I just didn't know.

Sometimes being a sidekick sucks, but being a teenager always sucks.

"Come on, Miles," I said, and turned to walk away.

"Later, Spuddy." Mandrake's voice was mocking, but quiet, so only I could hear him. He was a jerk, but not a big enough jerk to blow my secret identity.

"Even if you did use your lame powers," he

continued in a hushed voice, "you'd never be good enough to make *my* football team. Go run back to that vegetable-head you call a super-hero . . ."

Something snapped. I don't know if it was being humiliated in front of Prudence; or Charisma Kid mocking my powers; or if I just wanted to wipe that smug grin off his face; and I very seriously doubt it was because he insulted Pumpkin Pete, but something snapped.

The coach was throwing passes to wide receivers. I raced onto the field, not crazy-fast or super-power fast, but fast enough to turn a few heads. I zipped by the intended wide receiver, caught the coach's pass, and bolted for the end zone.

I spiked the ball. Mandrake gave a little snarl. My heart leaped with joy.

"I've never seen anyone run that fast!" the breathless coach huffed as he ran up to me. "What's your name, son?"

"Guy. Guy Martin."

The coach slapped me on the back. "Congratulations, Guy! You've just made the team!"

That was when the ground ripped open and the mole people attacked.

Chapter Fifteen

"I am the Mole Master, Master of Moles!" the little creature shouted from atop his giant worm. "You shall bow down before me! Grovel at the feet of your new master!"

One second I was being patted on the back by the coach, and the next I was in the middle of panic and screams as the Mole Master, Master of Moles, burst through the grassy earth on his giant worm. Football players and cheerleaders fled in terror. It only took me a few seconds to race behind the bleachers and whip my sidekick uniform from my backpack.

"Go get the League of Big Justice!" I told Miles before I raced out to stop the little villain that had erupted from under the earth . . . most likely to destroy us all or something. That seems to be what villains who erupt from under the earth always want to do.

The Mole Master was about two feet tall with a thick coat of short, dirty fur. He had small beady eyes and claws at the end of his curved hands. His nose was pink and it wrinkled every time he yelled.

His worm was about the size of a 747, without the wings and tail. And it probably couldn't fly, either.

"All you dirtless ones must bow down before the Mole Master, Master of Moles! I have come to conquer this neighborhood!" he shouted.

"This neighborhood? Don't you mean you've come to conquer the world?" I asked. Not that I wanted to encourage him to conquer the world, but it just seemed odd.

"The world?!" he gasped. "What would I do with the world? Sure, it'd be so nice at first, but then what? Huh? I'll tell you!"

"Wait!" I yelled back. "I really *don't* want to know."

I am so stupid! Never give a supervillain a chance to rant. If a supervillain ever made an outline of their attack plan, it would say:

STAGE 1
ATTACK

STAGE 2
RANT

STAGE 3
CONQUER WORLD

STAGE 4
RANT MORE

STAGE 5
EAT PUDDING

And don't ask me to explain the whole pudding thing. I'm just telling it like it is.

"Sure, all of you would live in fear of my awesome power of dirt! But . . . soon enough you'd start complaining and whining about pollution or the quality of your schools. 'O Mole Master, Master of Moles, our taxes are too high.' 'O Mole Master, Master of Moles, there's too much violence on TV.' 'O Mole Master, Master of Moles, it's no fun being slaves in your dirt mines.' Bah! Who needs it!? I have enough headaches from living underground!"

"What's so bad about living underground?" I asked.

"What's so bad?!? *THERE'S DIRT EVERY-WHERE!* There's dirt in your water! There's dirt in your food! There's dirt in your hair and your phone and your pudding and your underwear! It buries your TV during *Friends* and then you have to wait a *whole week* to see if Ross and Rachel get back together!"

"So you're here to conquer the neighborhood?"

"You got that right! Convenient freeway access, a local cineplex, nearby schools, slaves for my dirt mines. And best of all . . . no dirt! I conquer the neighborhood, hold onto it for a few years, and then turn a sweet profit when I sell! My plan is flawless! Do you hear me? Flawless!" The Mole Master cackled with glee.

"Oh yeah? I can think of one flaw!" I shouted back.

He stopped laughing. "Is it dirt?"

"No! It's me!"

"Are you made of dirt?"

"No."

"Then you are powerless to stop me!" He began to cackle again. "If you were made of dirt then I would say, 'Oh no! Oh no! You're made of dirt? Please don't fall into my glass of Tang! I just want one glass of Tang without dirt in it! JUST ONE!' But you have already admitted that you are in fact *not* made of dirt!"

"Maybe I lied," I countered. "Maybe I really *am* made of dirt."

"You are blue and dirt is brown. If you were made of dirt, you would be brown and not blue. But you are blue and not brown. Therefore you are not dirt. Haha! I have run circles around you logically!" The Mole Master plopped back slightly on his worm, a satisfied grin on his furry face.

"I'm not blue," I pointed out. "That's just the color of my costume."

"I will not be tricked by your dirtless ways! You are just as stupid as a monkey! But you are not a monkey, because monkeys are brown and, as we have already established, you are not brown but blue!" He scratched his furry chin. "Are monkeys made of dirt?"

"No."

"Whew! That's a relief!" He sighed and scanned the empty football field. "Well, since the other dirtless ones have fled, you'll have to meet your doom by yourself!"

Chapter Sixteen
Meeting My Doom

"Attack, my mole legions! Attack the dirtless ones! I, Mole Master, Master of Moles, command you to attack!"

He stood on the giant worm's back and thrust his stubby hand forward. My muscles tensed. I prepared myself for the invasion force that would pour forth from the enormous hole made by the worm. The Mole Master cackled with euphoric glee, and then, the first mole appeared over the lip of the hole.

The mole was an ordinary, furry little mole with cute whiskers. He lumbered toward me through the dirt. I thought I could hear him growling.

"*That's* your invasion force?" I asked as the little mole began gnawing on my boot.

"The first of millions! Millions!" he yelled back. "They shall gnaw their way to victory! Flee before them, dirtless one! Fleeeeee!"

The little mole at my feet stopped gnawing and wrinkled his nose.

"Gnaw, my mole legions! Gnaaaaaaaaw!" The Mole Master stopped. He looked down the hole, then checked the watch on his wrist. "Any minute now."

I shooed away the little mole at my feet. He growled and then scampered back toward the enormous hole. "Where are my legions?" the Mole Master shouted down to the lone mole. The tiny mole made a few grunts and wrinkled its nose again.

"What do you mean they're not coming? Didn't they get the memo? We're invading today!"

The tiny mole squealed.

"Digging in the dirt? Why are they digging in the dirt when we're supposed to be invading?"

"I thought moles liked digging in the dirt," I commented.

"Mind your own business! This is between me and my legions!" He scratched his head and thought for a moment. He finally shrugged his shoulders. "Oh well. I'll just have to destroy the dirtless ones myself."

He gave a little kick to the huge worm. It reared back, then slid from the hole. Its enormous body slammed into the field. I raced out of the way as it smashed through the bleachers and roared.

"Speedy! Speedy!" It was Miles! He was back, and hopefully with the League of Big Justice! The Mole Master, Master of Moles, and his legion of moles, or maybe it would be better to say his legion of *mole*, didn't seem like much of a threat.

The huge worm that destroyed everything in its path was another story.

"Did you find the League of Big Justice?" I called out as I dove clear of falling debris.

"Sort of . . ."

"What do you mean, 'sort of'?"

"I told Pumpkin Pete there was an emergency, and he turned on the TV news to see what was happening," Miles informed me.

"Didn't you get anybody? I need help!"

"Uh . . . I *did* manage to get someone . . ."

I finally saw him. He stepped in front of Miles like a noble, stinky statue.

"Although we are bitter enemies, sidekick, on this day, we fight side by side! So speaks Commander Farto: The Human Stink Bomb! Let evil tremble before my awesome stench! Run before my mighty stink! Cower before my rankness, villain, for on this day it shall be I, Commander Farto: The Human Stink Bomb, who wins the day! By the power of gas, I command you to stop!"

That was when the worm ate him.

Chapter Seventeen
Burp!

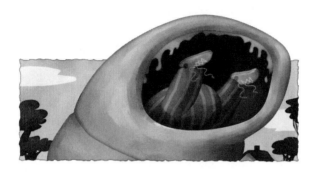

Burp!

So much for Commander Farto: The Human Stink Bomb.

Chapter Eighteen
The Chapter After Burp!

"Oh yes! I'll have a lovely little home with a hedge and a garden. And a pond! Yes! A nice pond with fish! But no dirt! No dirt, do you hear me? And no hummingbird feeder! Let those stupid birds find their own food!" the Mole Master shouted as he rode his monster worm through the once-tranquil neighborhood streets. But I don't think anyone was listening. They were too busy running away and screaming in terror.

"Don't run away screaming! You'll all be so happy as slaves in my dirt mines! I promise you'll only be digging the best dirt!"

I had been chasing after the worm, making

sure no one got hurt. It had smashed through the school, which I admit I didn't do much to prevent, but now the Mole Master was leading it on a rampage through the city streets.

"Sidekicks: Assemble!" I heard a voice cry out behind me. I turned to see Charisma Kid leading the Sidekicks toward the carnage. I had wondered where he had gone. At least he was smart enough to get help.

Well, maybe not *help*, exactly.

"Don't worry," Exact Change Kid immediately said as they ran up. He was carrying the Sidekick Official Box of Secret Ballotness and Due Process. "'Sidekicks: Assemble!' isn't the official battle cry yet, so you didn't miss your chance to vote. We just wanted to see how it felt in the field. You know, battle-test it."

"It's great," I replied, not really caring. "We need to stop —"

"'It's great'? So . . . is that a 'yes' vote?" Exact Change Kid asked.

"I'm not voting! I'm saying we have to stop the Mole Master, Master of Moles, before he destroys everything!"

"I don't think that was on the ballot," Spice Girl said. "And it's a little long to remember."

"Who cares about the ballot? We have to stop evil!" I urged.

"Just because voting is your right, Speedy, doesn't mean you should just throw it away," Exact Change Kid chided me.

The giant worm turned and smashed three houses.

"Too much dirt! And no breakfast nook!" the Mole Master shouted, and directed his worm toward some other homes down the street.

"Okay! I vote 'no'!" I said, giving in.

"See! I told you he would!" Boom Boy huffed. "Why are you such a troublemaker?"

"ME? I'm a troublemaker? What about the little guy on the giant worm destroying the city?"

"He's not the one who voted 'no.'" Boom Boy rolled his eyes. "Passing the blame onto someone else. Real mature."

"I'm not trying to be a troublemaker." I looked over Boom Boy's shoulder and saw the worm crush ten more cars. "It's just that . . . it seems like you guys always have some urgent thing going on that has nothing to do with the *real* urgent thing that's going on."

"Now we're just 'you guys'?" Exact Change Kid complained. "So much for being teammates!"

"I told you," Boom Boy shrugged. "Trouble-maker."

"Ma pam mam," Boy-in-the-Plastic-Bubble Boy agreed.

"Maybe Speedy can vote on our battle cry after we stop the invasion?" Spelling Beatrice suggested, a dim bulb of common sense in a dark room of insanity.

"Notice how the two without 'lad' or 'lass' or 'boy' or 'kid' in their names gang up on the rest of us?" Earlobe Lad whispered.

"Oh, I see how it is," Boom Boy began. "Gang up on Boom Boy so his battle cry, 'Sidekicks: Assemble!,' loses! So that's how it's going to be, is it?"

"But we're not ganging up on you, Boom Boy," Spelling Beatrice stated.

"'Cause you know, if you do . . . if you do . . . I swear, I'll blow myself up!" Boom Boy doubled over as if someone had just punched him in the gut. He tightened his stomach muscles and clenched his teeth even tighter.

That was when the worm ate him.

"Run away!" Exact Change Kid yelled.

The Sidekicks raced for cover as the worm smashed into the ground and created another huge hole, disappearing into the earth with the Mole Master.

"Where's the League of Big Justice?" I asked Spelling Beatrice urgently.

"They're doing the ribbon-cutting at the grand opening of Tar Pit World. Don't you remember how King Justice kept saying he was 'gonna get sticky'?"

"All of them went? Isn't someone on monitor duty?"

"Yeah. Pumpkin Pete," Spelling Beatrice informed me. "We tried to tell him it was an emergency, but he said he was too busy watching some emergency on the TV news."

"Pete'll never call them, will he?" I knew the answer before I even asked the question.

"I don't think so. He was wearing his Super Pumpkin Slippers and asked us to pick up some Chinese food on the way home."

"Maybe Boom Boy can still blast the worm with his laser eyes? Or Earlobe Lad can use his sweat powers!" Spice Girl suggested.

"That was just a story they told those girls at Pizza World!" I informed her.

"I knew that, silly!" Spice Girl claimed. She paused for a moment and thought. "Does that mean Exact Change Kid isn't really a stupid alien who was sent to Earth because he was so stupid?"

I turned back to Spelling Beatrice. "So it's just me, you, Spice Girl, Boy-in-the-Plastic-Bubble Boy, Exact Change Kid, Earlobe Lad, and Charisma Kid?"

Before Spelling Beatrice could answer, the worm came back, erupting from the earth, creating another massive hole, and eating Earlobe Lad and Charisma Kid in the process.

"Uh . . . make that me, you, Spice Girl, Boy-in-the-Plastic-Bubble Boy and Exact Change —"

I heard a giant *burp*.

"Err . . . forget about Exact Change Kid."

Spelling Beatrice and I were about to devise a plan when I saw it. Down one of the fifty-foot-wide holes, hanging from a pointed rock, was a lone blue pom-pom.

Prudence's blue pom-pom.

She was down there. Somewhere. In the darkness. In the dirt. In the bowels of the earth surrounded by a legion of angry, gnawing moles.

"Stop the worm," I said to Spelling Beatrice. "I have a life to save."

I raced down the hole and into the silence of the awaiting darkness.

Chapter Nineteen
Evil Hates Dirt

"Welcome to my palace!" the Mole Master, Master of Moles, said to me the moment I ran into the large cavern.

I had flicked on my Sidekick Super Flashlight Accessory of Shininess, raced down the hole, and run through the silence of darkness for several minutes. Twists and turns, bends and curves, the great worm tunnel plummeted downward into the belly of the earth. Finally, I came to smaller passages, and then I found him.

"Nice, isn't it?" the Mole Master asked. "Only the best dirt, I assure you. I've had most of this dug all the way from Italy. Why, I've got an Italian dirt bed and a French dirt dining room set.

I've got a dirt Jacuzzi and a dirt throne with some wonderful dirt jewels. Simply smashing, isn't it?"

"I thought you hated dirt," I asked, scanning for Prudence.

"I DO! Look at this place! It's DIRT!" the Mole Master kicked a mound of dirt. "Have you brought me more dirt, hmmm? Perhaps you'd like to see my dirt mines?"

"I've come for the girl!" I stated.

"The girl? Is she made of dirt?"

"No! She's a . . . 'dirtless one' . . ."

"Then I probably fed her to Virgil." He noticed my blank stare. "The *worm*."

The words stabbed through my heart like a knife. I'd failed. No. Worse than that. I'd failed to save someone I cared for, someone who, if she even knew I was alive, would have counted on me to save her.

And I let her down. If she knew I existed, she'd probably be real disappointed in me right now.

"Attack, my mole legions! Attack the dirtless one! I, Mole Master, Master of Moles, command you to attack!" He thrust his stubby hand forward. My muscles tensed. I prepared myself for the attacking legions to pour forth from the darkness. The Mole Master cackled with euphoric glee, and then, the first mole appeared from behind the dirt throne. "Gnaw, my mole legions! Gnaaaaaaaw!" he screamed at the appearance of his lone mole warrior. He stopped, then looked into the darkness behind his throne, awaiting the flood of his mole hordes.

The tiny mole made a few grunts and wrinkled its nose. "What do you mean they're not coming? How can I gnaw my way to victory without my legions?"

The tiny mole squealed.

"What? They're tired of me ordering them around? I am the Mole Master, Master of Moles! Listen to the name! '*Master* of Moles!' It's not 'Mole Master, Hey I've Got Some Really Keen Suggestions for You Moles!' Did I say, 'Call me Mole Master, Head of the Round Table of Discussion for Moles?!' NO! I am the Mole Master, Master of Moles! Master! Master! *Master!* Go tell them their master *orders* them to gnaw!"

The little mole sighed and scurried off into the darkness. I can't speak mole, but I'm pretty sure he was swearing.

"This will just take a moment," he said to me. "Then we'll get back to gnawing you to death and making you bow down before me." He checked his watch and hummed to himself, then added, "Would you like something while you wait? Perhaps . . . oh, I don't know . . . some dirt?"

"I want to know what you did with Prudence!" I yelled back. I couldn't believe she was gone. There had to be something I could do.

"Go ask Virgil. He ate her, not me."

My head spun. It felt like my heart slammed down into my feet and pounded in my left pinky toe. I would bring the furball of terror and dirt to justice, that was for sure. No one, and I mean no one, eats Prudence Cane without answering to me.

The worm eating Charisma Kid, I wasn't so upset about. But Prudence was another story.

That was when I saw it — something moving behind the dirt throne. "Help me . . . ," a weak female voice pleaded.

"Prudence!" I shouted.

She stumbled out from behind the throne. Thick dirt covered her face, hair, and arms. She was dazed, but otherwise unhurt. She was happy to see another human. She looked at me and smiled.

"I'll save you, Prudence!" My heart raced from my little toe, swerved around my intestines, ricocheted off my liver, and finally plopped back in my chest, where it happily beat like a little heart that was happy to be beating someplace other than a pinky toe.

"You'll do no such thing!" the Mole Master warned, and stepped down from his throne. "This is my queen! She'll bake me cookies and we'll sit on the porch of my new dirt-free house and drink lemonade and laugh at all the dirt that isn't in our food!"

One thing I've never understood about su-pervillains that come from the ocean or under the earth is that they always show up yakking about how they're going to "crush the surface-dwellers," then they spot some pretty girl and want to make her their queen and suddenly all their "crushing" plans go out the window. You'll never catch "normal" supervillains looking for a queen. They want to rule the world all by them-selves. I suppose it *does* make things a whole lot simpler when you can rule the world with your cruel iron fist and not have to worry about being romantic and stuff.

"But she's a dirtless one!" I reminded him.

"No, she is not! She is the Mole Mistress, Mis-tress of Moles, and she is made of dirt! Look! She is brown and dirt is brown. If she were a dirtless one, she would be dirtless and not brown. But she is brown and not dirtless. Therefore she is made of dirt. Haha! Or . . . perhaps she's a monkey."

"But you hate dirt!"

The bushy little villain stamped his little mole feet. "You will not run circles around *me* logically! Now . . . go dig in my dirt mines, slave!"

"I'll never be your slave, Mole Master!"

"And you wonder why I don't conquer the earth? You're my only dirtless slave now, and all you do is complain, complain, complain! Imagine ruling a whole planet of you! 'O Mole Master, Master of Moles, the price of gasoline is too high!' 'O Mole Master, Master of Moles, there's too much traffic on the freeways!' 'O Mole Master, Master of Moles, your giant worm ate my parents!' Bah! Who needs it?"

Before he could say another word, I grabbed Prudence and raced toward the surface.

"Wait! Where are you going?" the crazy rodent called after me. "The dirt mines are the other way!"

Prudence is a lot slower than I am. Actually, everyone in the world is slower than me, which usually doesn't matter, except now I was racing for my life, for *two* lives. I did my best to carry Prudence. She was light as a feather. And blond. Did

I mention that? Blond hair, blond eyes, blond skin, blond —

"I offer you my hospitality! I offer you my dirt! And this is how you repay me? You steal my queen?" I heard a voice shout from the darkness behind me. "VIRGILLLLLLLLLLL!"

Let me stop this slingshot of fun for a moment, just to recap my life. I'm running through a dark tunnel while an overgrown mole who speaks English, mind you, stands on his dirt throne having a tantrum and shouting for his giant pet worm, Virgil, to come eat me because I stole his human queen.

I never realized it before, but there was some really freaky stuff going on under my city.

I could hear Virgil's roar as he broke through the wall of the throne room. I didn't know how long it would take for the Mole Master to climb up the giant worm, but if they caught me in this dark tunnel carrying Prudence, I was worm food for sure.

"Oh my gosh!" Prudence suddenly gasped as we neared the light of the surface. "You're a sidekick, aren't you?"

This was my chance. My big chance for her to finally notice me. I saved her life. I saved her from being a little furry creature's queen. I mean, that's just *got* to score me some major points! "Actually, yes, I am a sidekick," I said with a smile.

"Oh my gosh! Oh my gosh!" she gushed. "You know Charisma Kid!"

I really wondered if the Mole Master was still interested in having a queen.

Chapter Twenty
Holy Potatoes

The moment we got to the surface, I sent Prudence for cover.

"Tell Charisma Kid I said hi!" she yelled as she ran down the street to safety.

Odds were, I'd be the next between-meals snack for Virgil, so I probably would be able to deliver that message to Charisma Kid in person.

The ground shook and a thunderous sound blasted from the deep tunnel. I scanned the area for any of the Sidekicks. They were gone, all of them. I wasn't sure if they were hiding, in Virgil's stomach, or watching TV with Pumpkin Pete, but I knew that I'd have to face the danger alone.

Again.

How do you stop a giant worm? Think, Guy, think! With a giant fish? Yes! No! Where would I get a giant fish? Maybe a giant fishing hook? Great. I can probably get that at the same place I can find a giant fish. What do worms hate? Birds! Maybe I can find an army of pigeons and they can peck it to death!

The ground behind me erupted as Virgil burst from the earth, the Mole Master riding on his back. Earth and rock flew into the sky, and I tumbled down the outside of the newly formed mound.

"What have you done with my queen?" the Mole Master yelled from high atop the worm.

I think it may have been a rhetorical question because he didn't wait for an answer. Virgil dove at me, mouth open. Drool hung from his doughy mouth and the rotten stink of his breath reminded me of Commander Farto: The Human Stink Bomb's sad fate.

I raced behind a large oak tree at 42 miles per hour and easily dodged Virgil, but the worm turned and ripped the massive oak from the ground like it was a weed. Which I guess would've made me the tiny little bug that was hiding under the weed.

"You can't hide like a tiny little bug under a

weed!" The Mole Master laughed. "But don't worry! I'll be a kind master! Every year on your birthday, I'll give you a new shovel to dig in my dirt mines!"

"Sorry Mole Master, but I'm bringing you down!"

"Oh? Are you? Do you have a giant fish I don't know about? Or perhaps a giant fishhook?" he asked. "Until your army of pigeons shows up, tell me where my queen is or suffer the consequences!"

I can't say I really blame him. I mean, Prudence is pretty terrific and all. In fact, if I were a two-foot-tall mole, I'd be smitten with her, too, and —

Virgil lunged at me. I raced away, the huge worm hot on my tail, crushing everything in its path. This was no good. The longer I kept running away, the more damage Virgil was doing, and soon someone was going to get hurt.

And that someone would most likely be me.

Pumpkin Pete once told me that the three things every superhero needs are insurance, an agent, and a tailor. But I think the real thing every superhero needs is a plan. The longer I was a sidekick, the more I realized that no matter how fast I ran around, it just didn't solve *anything*. I had to use my head. I had to think. Think of the supervillain's weakness. Like that time the Sidekicks battled Captain Claustrophobia. We just tricked him into an elevator, and that battle was over real quick.

"Curses! You've discovered my secret weakness," Captain Claustrophobia cried as he hyperventilated into a paper bag while we rode up to the fiftieth floor.

I thought just having a super power would be all I needed. Who knew you actually had to *think* when you punched evil in the face. I thought all this would be more like TV wrestling.

I zipped around the corner and was nearly run over by the Pumpkinmobile. Pete screeched to a halt and rolled down the window.

"There you are! I've been looking all over for you!" Pete was actually happy to see me. And the funny thing was, I was happy to see him, too.

"Pete! You came!" I gasped, and looked back over my shoulder to see Virgil whip around the corner. "You've got to help me stop the Mole Master from taking over the neighborhood!"

"Stop who?" Pete asked.

"The Mole Master, Master of Moles!"

"Look, I don't know anything about your skin problem, but I've got a date tomorrow night and

I need someone to iron my Super Pumpkin Suit of Handsomeness. Didn't we already discuss that was part of your sidekick duty to — holy potatoes!" Pete finally saw Virgil barreling toward us. He slammed his foot on the gas pedal. "Pumpkin feets, don't fail me now!"

The back tires of the Pumpkinmobile burned rubber. I leaped through the open window on the passenger's side as Pete sped away.

"Why are you such a troublemaker?" Pete huffed.

"Me? *I'm* a troublemaker?" I protested. "I'm not the one on the giant worm destroying the city!"

"No, but you're the person the one on the giant worm destroying the city is *chasing*!"

The Pumpkinmobile skidded around a corner. "Out of the way, grandpa!" Pete shouted out the window. "Superhero coming through!"

If it weren't for the fact we were being chased by a monster worm and a two-foot-tall mole, I'd swear we were just going to pick up Pete's dry cleaning.

"Okay, kid! Where can we get a giant fish?" Pete asked as the Pumpkinmobile skidded around the next corner.

"Pete . . ." Now that I had a moment to think,

I realized what horrible things had happened. A lump grew in my throat as I searched for the right words. "I think the worm ate the Sidekicks."

"All of 'em?" Pete gasped.

"Yes." The lump became a mountain.

"Even *my* sidekick?"

"No, Pete. *I'm* your sidekick."

Pete's shoulders slumped. "Oh. Then I probably can't get a new one, can I?" Pete sat in silence for a moment, his fingers tapping on the Pumpkinmobile's steering wheel. "So I guess the worm didn't eat *all* of them, now did it?"

The only idea worse than running around while a giant worm chased you, destroying everything, was being driven around while a giant worm chased you, destroying everything. I knew it was a long shot, but I had to try. "Pete . . . maybe now would be a good time to teach me the secrets of the mysterious Ways of the Pumpkin . . ."

"Okay. Sure. Here's secret number one: Always have a super distraction."

"Do you have one now?" I asked.

"*Do* I!" Pete's viney finger stabbed at the dashboard and hit the red button for the ejector seat. The next thing I knew, I was sailing through the air like a Wiffle ball hit by King Kong.

Sometimes I really hate Pumpkin Pete.

I landed hard. A sharp pain stabbed through my hip. I rolled to my feet, but it was too late. Virgil was hovering over me, his mouth open like an enormous black hole. He blocked out the sun.

"As you are slowly digested in Virgil's stomach, know that you shall always have a special place in my heart as my very first dirtless slave. I will always cherish the dirt you dug for me," the Mole Master called down.

"I never dug any dirt for you!"

"Hmmm," he rubbed his fuzzy chin. "You're right. Perhaps I won't miss you that much after all."

Virgil's mouth came down upon me like a great blanket. I prepared to be covered in goopy worm saliva while being slowly digested in Virgil's squishy stomach.

Chapter Twenty-One
Covered in Goopy Worm Saliva While Being Slowly Digested in Virgil's Squishy Stomach

Actually, that didn't happen.

Chapter Twenty-Two
What Actually Happened Instead of Getting Covered in Goopy Worm Saliva While Being Slowly Digested in Virgil's Squishy Stomach

Virgil's head slammed into the asphalt, but I wasn't there. I was in the sky again, zipping to safety — being *carried* to safety. My feet touched ground again about three hundred yards away from the Mole Master. I turned to see who my rescuer was.

I saw brown. I saw a man with these things that looked like featherless wings under his arms. His head was covered with a sleek armored mask that protruded slightly at the nose and brow, almost like a bird. Only his mouth was visible. I saw him for an instant, and then, as quickly as he had swooped down to save my life, again, he shot into the sky, again, little more than a brown bolt.

"Hey! Hey!" I yelled after him. "Who are you?!?"

Just like he did after he saved me from Dr. Robot, my mysterious benefactor disappeared as if he had only existed in my dreams.

"I wish I could be *his* sidekick," I said aloud, thinking of how Pete had ejected me from the Pumpkinmobile to get Virgil off his tail.

And speaking of Virgil . . .

"Have you come back to dig more dirt in my dirt mines?" the Mole Master called out as he rode Virgil closer. "Grovel before me, dirtless one! Grovel before the Mole Master, Master of —!"

"No! I've come back to stop you. I've come back to save the Sidekicks."

"Save them? Check your watch, slave! You're about thirty-minutes-past-lunchtime too late!"

I had been given a second chance. It was time to stop running around. It was time to be a hero. If I could be saved against impossible odds, maybe the Sidekicks could be as well. I couldn't give up. It was like King Justice said: Where there is hope, where there is strength, the impossible can become the ordinary.

So what if he was talking about winning the three-legged race at the League of Big Justice Super Family Picnic of Potluck.

I couldn't let the Sidekicks down. They may

drive me nuts, but they are my friends . . . my family. A family of mutated oddities with huge ears, excellent grammar, exact change, and plastic bubbles, but a family nonetheless.

Yeah, I know I said that already, but I had to think of some good reason why I was trying to save Charisma Kid.

It was time to end the Mole Master's wormy ride of terror.

"You want your queen back? I'll show you where she is!" I zipped in the opposite direction, and he ordered Virgil to follow.

I did my best to avoid places where people would be. I knew where I had to go. Luckily for me, Spelling Beatrice had said something earlier that gave me an idea. Virgil was fast, but he couldn't slither 100 miles per hour. Fighting him was one thing; letting him chase me was much safer.

In a matter of minutes, I had reached my destination: the grand opening of Tar Pit World. Sure, the League of Big Justice may still be there, and maybe even King Justice's Giant Ribbon-Cutting Scissors of Ceremonial Justice, but even if they weren't, the tar still was.

The Mole Master watched me stop before the edge of the tar pits. "If you intend to be my slave, there'll have to be a whole lot less running and a whole lot more digging."

"I'll never be your slave!" I said defiantly.

"I'm not listening!" the Mole Master replied. "Never!"

"I can't hear you! La-la-la-la-la!"

"You'll never have that house with a hedge and a garden!" I taunted.

"Did you hear something, Virgil? Not me!"

"No queen to make you iced tea —"

"It was lemonade!" the Mole Master burst out, then realized he had "heard" me. "Gaaah! Curse you, dirtless one! You've tricked me with your dirtless ways!"

"Then come and get me, mole man."

"Mole *Master*!" he corrected.

"You're no master. You're just an overgrown rodent with a giant worm. You couldn't even be master to a gopher!"

The Mole Master nearly erupted with anger. He kicked Virgil's sides and the worm lunged forward, mouth agape. "I wish you *were* made of dirt so I could hate you even more!" he screamed at me as Virgil arced through the air.

I raced to the side, but Virgil was too wide. As he smashed into the tar pits, the side of his leathery skin sideswiped me and sent me tumbling into the black, sticky goo as well. As Virgil thrashed about in the tar pit and sunk ever deeper, he threatened to squash me. I struggled to move away, but the more I moved, the deeper I sank as well.

I don't know if sinking slowly under a lake of tar is better than getting squished quickly, but I wasn't about to wait around. I stabbed my hands into the tar and pulled them out covered in the sticky black gunk. A thunderous roar bellowed from Virgil's mouth as the monster worm grew tired of fighting the thick resin. I slapped my hands against the creature's side, kicked furiously with my super-powered legs, and pulled myself from the deadly tar. With the gummy substance covering most of my body, I scaled the worm's side like a tiny black fly.

"So! Have you come to kneel before the awesome might of the Mole Master, Master of Moles?" he shouted at me the moment I climbed to the top.

"Would you shut up already with that?" I answered.

"You know, you have a lot to learn about being a slave," the Mole Master informed me. "Like, lesson number one: Never foil your master's plan to rule the neighborhood!"

"Sorry, Mole Master, your great kingdom is nothing but dirt." I *had* to say it.

"Is it now? My plans may have hit a small bump, but at least I'll be able to crawl back under the earth knowing that I destroyed you!"

He let out a feral growl, bared his mole claws, and charged at me. As he was about to pounce, I grabbed him by the nape of his neck and lifted him off the ground. He was still only two feet tall. He swung wildly, fists whooshing through the air. After a minute of swinging, he stopped, his body heaving with deep breaths.

"Okay," he huffed, trying to catch his breath. "We'll call it a tie."

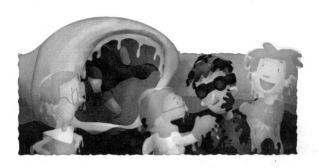

"There's one more left, and boy-o! Is he the mother! Of! All! Stinkies!" King Justice waved at his super nose with one hand as he gently placed Boom Boy on the ground next to the other sidekicks.

"Good thing you came when you did, King Justice, sir," Boom Boy spoke up, shaking the thick mucus from his arms. "I thought I'd have to blow myself up to save the others."

"A good hero knows when to blow up himself, and when to blow up someone else. I think you'll find it wise to always try to blow up someone else first, my young firecracker." King Justice patted Boom Boy on the back and walked back into Virgil's dark, slobbery mouth. "Worry not, flatulent one! The King is on his way!"

Unable to break free of the tar pit, Virgil had finally stopped resisting. The truckload of tranquilizers that the League of Big Justice had fed him also had a calming effect. Now he lay there, snoring happily, his mouth propped open like the archway to a giant fun house.

I discovered one good thing today. When you're very small and get swallowed by something very enormous with a slow digestive tract, you end up in a stomach about the size of a gymnasium. Sure, you get covered with all kinds of worm guts and gooey liquids I don't even want to think about, but it's a heck of a lot better to come back out of the mouth instead of going out the other end, if you know what I mean.

And luckily worms don't have teeth, even monster worms, so none of the Sidekicks even got chewed. I mean, I suppose they could *still* have been gummed to death, but that's just a chance we heroes take.

Not being gummed to death. Just death in a general sense.

"I'm glad everybody's okay!" I said to the goo-covered sidekicks. I noticed Charisma Kid wasn't there anymore. The idea of being saved by me probably got under his skin as much as the idea of me saving Charisma Kid got under mine. I think both of us were thankful for a quick exit on his part.

"Thanks for saving us, Speedy," Exact Change Kid spoke first. "Sorry about all the trouble we caused about voting for 'Sidekicks: Assemble.'"

"Hey, don't worry about it. It's a cool battle cry."

Exact Change Kid looked to the ground. He shuffled his foot. "So . . . is that a 'yes' vote?"

I rolled my eyes and shook my head. "Do we have to do this now?"

"There he goes, already causing trouble." Boom Boy threw up both his hands. Thick globs of worm saliva sailed through the air and splatted on Boy-in-the-Plastic-Bubble Boy's Giant Hamster Ball of Justice.

"I'm not trying to cause trouble! I just —"

"Could you please try to not try to cause trouble a little more quietly, then?" Earlobe Lad gasped. He slopped two mucus-covered hands over his ears. "At least I didn't have to listen to your yapping in that stomach."

"Speedy just saved our lives!" Spelling Beatrice defended. "Give him a break."

"Five minutes out of the stomach and those

two are already ganging up on us," Boom Boy warned the others.

"Maaa pam mam ma . . . ," Boy-in-the-Plastic-Bubble Boy added.

"I wouldn't doubt it," Exact Change Kid said. "But, you know, if he wants to be just 'Speedy,' we just have to respect that until I finally get that petition printed up."

"I don't care how many petitions you sign, I am not changing my name to Speedy Kid, Speedy Lad, Speedy Boy, Speedy Jr., or Speedy Little Guy!"

"How about Speedy Lass?" Spice Girl suggested.

"No!"

"So Speedy Gal is probably out, too?" She crossed her arms in a huff.

Just as I was about to ask King Justice to put the Sidekicks back into the worm's stomach, The Stain and Ms. Mime came by, dragging a handcuffed Mole Master with them.

"This is your last chance to bow down before me, slave!" he yelled at me. "I won't ask you again! I swear! I'm going to count to three!"

"Sorry Mole Master, I don't bow for anyone," I said in a gritty voice.

"Or add 'Lad' to his name," Boom Boy called out from behind me.

"You think you've won, don't you? Well gnaw on this: I am told they'll take me to a place called 'prison'! It's made of concrete! There's no dirt there! I'll have no dirt in my food! I'll have no dirt in my bed! I'll have my own room and dirt won't even be allowed to visit! Not even during visiting hours! So tell me this: Who has truly won the battle on this day? I ask you that, slave! Who has won? Hahahahahaha!" He paused for a moment. "It's you, isn't it?"

The Stain and Ms. Mime led the Mole Master to the League of Big Justice SUV of Justice and Gas Guzzleness. They opened the door and carefully lifted him inside.

"Okay, when we arrive at the prison, bow down before me just a little bit," he said to The Stain and Ms. Mime. "You know, just to impress the other prisoners."

It was late and I was exhausted. It took hours to get all the tar off me, but my Spandex Speedy outfit wasn't so lucky. It was probably time for a new one anyway. That one had started to get some pretty nasty pit stains.

With all the Sidekicks safe and as irritating as ever, the mystery of my enigmatic benefactor really began to eat at me. Not that I minded being saved from becoming a low-cal snack to a giant worm, but I just had to know who that guy was, or if he even was a guy. Or even human. In my business you can never be too sure.

I walked into the League of Big Justice Hall of

Heroes of Big Justice. Everybody who had ever been a member of the League of Big Justice was immortalized in stone. The janitor, Captain Vacuum, was cleaning the marble floors with his Push Broom of Righteousness.

Captain Vacuum wasn't a member of the League of Big Justice. He didn't have a super power, either. He just liked to call himself Captain Vacuum because it impressed "the ladies."

"Evening, Speedy," Captain Vacuum greeted me.

"Hello Joh — I mean Captain Vacuum. How goes the fight against grime?"

"Never-ending, kiddo. Never-ending."

I left Captain Vacuum to his battle against the forces of mildew and strolled down the long line of statues. They were all here: The Oxymoron. Barnacle Bill. The Snot Rocketeer. Slappy the Clown. Statue Man. Captain Sweat Man. And so many more.

"Hey, what're you staring at?" Statue Man suddenly asked.

"Sorry. I thought you were a statue," I explained.

"I don't stare at you while you fight crime!"

"Fight crime?" I questioned. "You were just standing on your pedestal acting like a statue."

"When was the last time you heard of a felony being committed in the League of Big Justice Hall of Heroes of Big Justice?"

"Uh . . . never?"

"Then I guess I'm doing a darn good job, huh?" Statue Man crossed his arms and sneered.

I left him to battle evil and strolled further down the hall, inspecting each statue to see if any looked like the brown hero who had saved me. I passed the final statue of Garlic Gal at the end of the long hall and came to a piece of notebook paper taped to the wall. On it was a crayon drawing of Captain Vacuum.

"He came again, didn't he?" a voice behind me asked.

I turned to face King Justice. "How . . . how did you know?"

"Why else would you be here? It's practically a museum," King Justice replied.

"I like museums!" I quickly tried to cover.

King Justice cocked one mighty brow.

"Okay. I hate them," I admitted.

"I often come here myself. To understand the past is to understand the future, my museum-hating pal. And since Statue Man has been on patrol, I can't! Think! Of a! Safer! Place!"

"You know who he is, don't you?" I cut straight to the question and even surprised myself at my courage. "The hero who keeps saving me?"

"You know, I was a sidekick once," King Justice began.

"You?"

"Yes . . . of course I was only called Prince Justice then, but I was a sidekick to the greatest hero of all."

He was a sidekick to the greatest hero of all? I thought he *was* the greatest hero of all.

King Justice became more solemn than I had ever seen him. Even more solemn than the time Pumpkin Pete tried to do the League of Big Justice's laundry and shrank King Justice's last Spandex outfit two full sizes. *That* was one day evil will not soon forget.

King Justice led me to a large door. He pulled off one glove and slapped a large, noble hand on the laser scanner. A bright green light passed over his fingertips, and the door opened.

"These are my private quarters," he explained.

"Wow. Kinda like a sanctum sanctorum?"

"I like to call it my Happy Place of Thinking and Satellite TV."

I looked around the room. It was modest, but built for comfort; built for a king. Then something on the wall caught my attention. It wasn't another crayon drawing of Captain Vacuum. It was a picture; an old picture of King Justice and the man in brown.

And then it hit me.

"You were *his* sidekick?"

"He taught me everything I know. He was the reason I founded the League of Big Justice. Everything I am, I owe to him. He called himself 'The Strike.'"

"Why didn't he join the League of Big Justice?" I asked.

"We were a team. A great team. And then one day, twelve years ago, he disappeared. Without warning. Without a trace. All he left me was this note . . ."

King Justice opened a drawer and pulled out an old, folded piece of paper. It was fragile. The creases were splitting, as if the note had been opened and read a thousand times. I gently unfolded it, careful not to damage King Justice's precious memento. I read the note, hoping for the slightest clue.

"It's a grocery list," I finally said.

"Is it? Or is it a code? A cry for help? The coordinates of where he's being held captive?" King Justice clarified.

"No. I think it's just a grocery list." I handed the note back to King Justice.

"See, we had these decoder rings, and I lost mine. After all those years as partners, he wouldn't leave me a grocery list! I lost my decoder ring and . . ." His voice trailed off.

"I'm sorry, King Justice. Maybe . . . maybe . . ." I didn't know what to say. I saw cracks in the perfect veneer of my idol and, much to my amazement, saw the man showing through; a man who, no matter how many times he had saved the world without asking for a single thing in return, had lived for twelve years with the fear that his own idol never cared. "I'm sure you're right about the code."

There was a moment of silence between us, an awkward silence during which King Justice puffed out his chest and sealed the cracks from human eyes.

"Why is he back after all this time? What do you think he wants?" I asked.

"Revenge. Revenge against the world that turned its back on him. Revenge against any who looked upon him and laughed. Revenge against us all." King Justice paused for a moment. "Oh, wait. That's Captain Vacuum."

"Maybe he wants to talk with you," I suggested. "Or maybe he wants to join the League of Big Justice."

"Or maybe . . . he's looking for a new sidekick," King Justice countered.

I went white.

I sat by myself in front of the League of Big Justice. There was too much information swirling through my brain to go home. What could all this mean? Why did The Strike disappear twelve years ago, and why is he back? What does the grocery list mean? Why does Captain Vacuum want revenge?

"Hey! I thought I recognized you!" Pete spouted and slapped me on the back. "So . . . so . . . good to see you're still . . ."

"Alive?" I finished.

"Yeah, yeah," Pete agreed.

There was an awkward pause. Pete looked at

the ground and shuffled one foot on the pavement.

"You're probably wondering how I escaped the Mole Master, Master of Moles, and Virgil . . ."

"How you did who to what?" Pete replied.

"How I escaped the giant worm."

"Nah. Not really. You seem to be real good at that stuff. But I *was* wondering if you'd iron my suit before you went home tonight."

"I have a test to study for at school tomorrow!"

"Didn't we already discuss that ironing was part of your sidekick duty?"

I let out a long sigh. I was about to take the iron from Pete's hand, when the League of Big Justice was suddenly attacked!

Well, not attacked exactly. I recognized the supervillain from the League of Big Justice Files of Big Justice. He was the dreaded Mimic! He strutted up to Pumpkin Pete and me, eager for battle.

"What do you want?" Pete asked.

"What do *you* want?" The Mimic replied.

"I asked you first!" Pete spat.

"I asked *you* first!" The Mimic replied.

"Stop doing that!" Pete yelled.

"Stop *doing* that!" The Mimic replied.

I sat on the curb and dropped my head into my hands.

"I said stop it!" Pete yelled.

"*I* said stop it!" The Mimic replied.

"Don't make me use my Pumpkin Powers!" Pete yelled.

"Don't make me use *my* Pumpkin Powers!" The Mimic replied.

"You don't have Pumpkin Powers!" Pete yelled.

"*You* don't have Pumpkin Powers!" The Mimic replied.

It was going to be a long night.

Author Bios
Biographies of the Authors!

Dan Danko attributes his love of comic books to his childhood belief that he's from another planet. To this day, he has yet to be proven wrong.

Dan lists one of his greatest accomplishments as being fluent enough in Japanese to speak to a dim-witted seven-year-old. If Dan isn't watching Lakers' games, you'll find him traveling to any country that has a traveler's advisory from the U.S. State Department — much to his mother's dismay.

He's the tall one.

Tom Mason's love of comic books and all things superhero-y began when he had the flu and his parents bought him a stack of comics and sent him to the doctor.

When he's not selling his family's heirlooms on eBay or scuba diving off the California coast, he enjoys playing horseshoes with a long list of celebrities, all of whom once appeared on *The Love Boat*.

He's the cute one.

Dan and **Tom** are former editors and writers for Malibu and Marvel Comics, and they have also written for the TV series *Malcolm in the Middle* and *Rugrats*. They've been story editors on *Pet Alien* and on Nickelodeon's *Brothers Flub*.

Their combined height is twelve feet, one inch.

P.S. And they still read comic books!